W9-DDA-599

Learning to Read, Step by Step!

Ready to Read Preschool–Kindergarten
• big type and easy words • rhyme and rhythm • picture clues
For children who know the alphabet and are eager to begin reading.

Reading with Help Preschool–Grade 1
• basic vocabulary • short sentences • simple stories
For children who recognize familiar words and sound out new words with help.

Reading on Your Own Grades 1–3
• engaging characters • easy-to-follow plots • popular topics
For children who are ready to read on their own.

Reading Paragraphs Grades 2–3
• challenging vocabulary • short paragraphs • exciting stories
For newly independent readers who read simple sentences with confidence.

Ready for Chapters Grades 2–4
• chapters • longer paragraphs • full-color art
For children who want to take the plunge into chapter books but still like colorful pictures.

STEP INTO READING® is designed to give every child a successful reading experience. The grade levels are only guides. Children can progress through the steps at their own speed, developing confidence in their reading, no matter what their grade.

Remember, a lifetime love of reading starts with a single step!

This book is for Shelby
—A.J.H.

Text copyright © 2003 by Anna Jane Hays. Illustrations copyright © 2003 by Valeria Petrone. All rights reserved under International and Pan-American Copyright Conventions. Published in the United States by Random House Children's Books, a division of Random House, Inc., New York, and simultaneously in Canada by Random House of Canada Limited, Toronto.

www.randomhouse.com/kids

Library of Congress Cataloging-in-Publication Data
Hays, Anna Jane. The pup speaks up / by Anna Jane Hays ; illustrated by Valeria Petrone — 1st ed.   p.   cm. — (Step into reading.) "Step 1 book."
SUMMARY: After Bo and Pal, his silent new puppy, go for a walk and hear the various sounds of animals and objects around them, Pal finally speaks up.
ISBN 0-375-81232-6 (trade) — ISBN 0-375-91232-0 (lib. bdg.)
[1. Animal sounds—Fiction. 2. Sound—Fiction. 3. Dogs—Fiction. 4. Pets—Fiction. 5. Animals—Fiction.] I. Petrone, Valeria, ill. II. Title. III. Series. PZ7.H314917 Pu 2003 [E]—dc21
2002004585

Printed in the United States of America   10 9 8 7 6 5 4 3 2 1   First Edition

STEP INTO READING, RANDOM HOUSE, and the Random House colophon are registered trademarks of Random House, Inc.

The Pup Speaks Up

A Phonics Reader

by Anna Jane Hays

illustrated by Valeria Petrone

Random House 🏠 New York

Bo has a new pal.

Happy day!

"Hello!" says Bo.

"What do you say?"

The pup just wags
his tail.

Bo and Pal
go for a walk.
"What do you say?"
Bo asks a duck.

"Quack," says the duck.

"Honk," goes a truck.

"What do you say?"
Bo asks a bee.

"Buzz," says the bee.

"Buzz like me."

"Tick tock,"
goes a clock.

"Chug, chug,"

goes a tug.

A train calls,

"Choo choo!"

A baby cries,
"Boo-hoo!"

A rooster crows,
"Cock-a-doodle-do!"

An owl hoots,
"Hoo hoo! Hoo hoo!"

"What do you say?"

Bo asks Pal.

Pal just runs

and chases his tail.

A chick says,
"Cheep."

"Baa, baa,"

says a sheep.

A happy pig says,
"Oink, oink, oink."

boink

boink

boink

A bouncy ball goes

boink, boink, boink.

"Ribbit," says a frog.

But not the dog.

"What do you say?"

Bo asks his pup.

This time Pal
just jumps up.

"Moo!" says a cow.
Look out now . . .

Here comes a cat!

It says,

"MEOW!"

The pup speaks up!
"BOW WOW WOW!"

29

Bo says, "WOW!"

Hooray!

What a happy day!